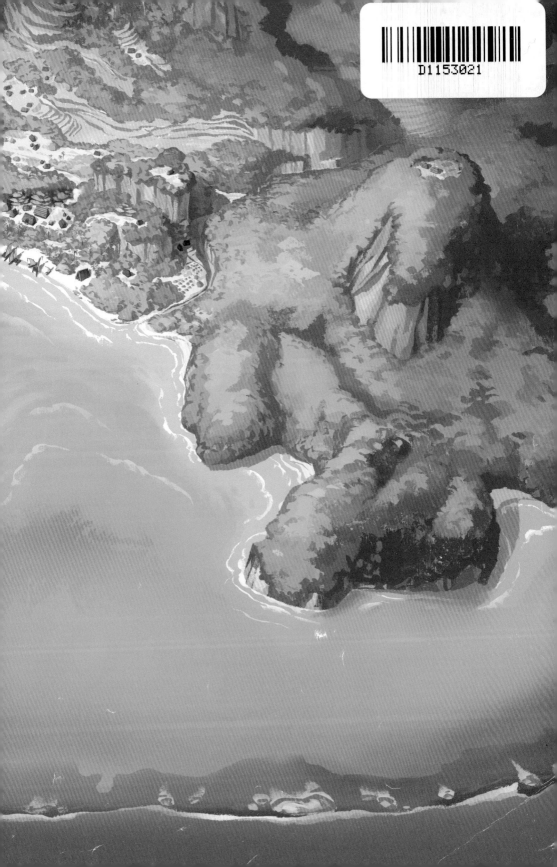

© 2017 Disney Enterprises, Inc.
Published by Hachette Partworks Ltd.
ISBN: 978-1-910360-64-4
Date of Printing: July 2017
Printed in Romania by Canale

Disney

H hachette

"A thousand years ago, the demigod Maui stole the heart of Te Fiti, the Mother of all the islands. Since then, the demon Te Kā has ruled the ocean. But one day, Maui will return Te Fiti's heart to her and save us all!" Gramma Tala finished telling the village children her story. Moana, her granddaughter, loved her grandmother's tales! But what Moana loved even more were the shells that the ocean washed up on the beach.

One day, a special wave delivered a gift – a green stone with a spiral pattern! Moana didn't know it, but it was the heart of the goddess Te Fiti. But as the little girl returned home, she accidentally dropped the stone.

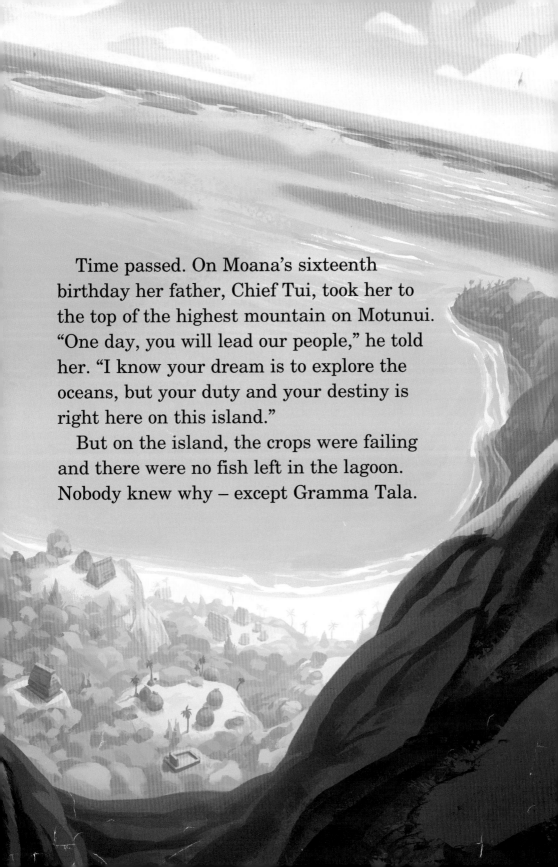

Time passed. On Moana's sixteenth birthday her father, Chief Tui, took her to the top of the highest mountain on Motunui. "One day, you will lead our people," he told her. "I know your dream is to explore the oceans, but your duty and your destiny is right here on this island."

But on the island, the crops were failing and there were no fish left in the lagoon. Nobody knew why – except Gramma Tala.

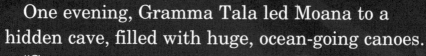

One evening, Gramma Tala led Moana to a
hidden cave, filled with huge, ocean-going canoes.
"So our ancestors were voyagers!" said Moana.
Gramma Tala nodded. "Do you remember this
stone that the wave gave you?" she asked. "I kept
it. It's the heart of Te Fiti. Somebody must journey
beyond the reef, find Maui and get him to return
Te Fiti's heart. If not, our island will be destroyed
by the demon Te Kā!"

That night, to the great sorrow of her family, Gramma Tala died.

Moana knew what she had to do. She took one of the boats from the cave and set sail to find Maui. Her sailing companion was Heihei, a funny little rooster.

Soon, a storm swept the boat to the island where Maui was stranded. Moana asked Maui to help her return the heart, but he refused. Then he tried to escape – on her boat!

With the ocean's help, Moana caught up with Maui.

"Why are you afraid of the heart?" she asked.

"It's cursed!" said Maui. "The moment I took it, I lost my hook and all my magic powers!"

Moana and Maui made a deal. She would help him get his hook back, if he helped her return the stone.

Just then, the Kakamora – fierce little creatures with coconut armour – appeared, climbing the rigging and throwing spears.

Luckily, Maui and Moana managed to fight them off and get away.

The pair sailed to a rocky spire – the entrance to Lalotai, the realm of monsters. According to Maui, this was where his hook was being held by Tamatoa, a monster who loved to collect shiny things.

Maui ordered Moana to stay on the boat, but she started climbing the spire. Maui looked doubtful.

"Of all the people on your island, why did they decide to send – um, how do I put this – you?"

"My people didn't send me," Moana replied. "The ocean did."

At the top of the spire, the demigod punched the ground, which opened to reveal a swirling vortex far below. Maui gave a warrior cry and jumped into the hole, with Moana following behind.

After a long fall to the bottom of the ocean and beyond, they landed in Lalotai. Now all they had to do was find Tamatoa...

Soon, they found a cave. Inside, on top of a huge mound of shiny treasure, Moana spotted Maui's fishhook.

But the mound turned out to be Tamatoa's shell – he was a giant crab!

As Moana distracted the monster, Maui snatched his fishhook back. The pair escaped and journeyed on to find Te Fiti.

Back at sea, Maui practised his rusty powers to turn himself into different creatures.

Finally, Te Fiti's island came into view. But suddenly the lava monster, Te Kā, rose up! Te Kā's fist came down towards the boat, but Maui

After the fight with the monster, Maui realised his hook was cracked. Maui felt he was powerless without it. In despair he shape-shifted into a hawk and flew away into the night sky.

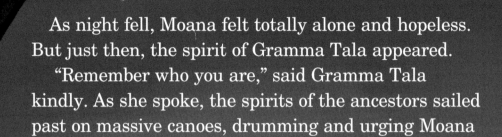

As night fell, Moana felt totally alone and hopeless. But just then, the spirit of Gramma Tala appeared.

"Remember who you are," said Gramma Tala kindly. As she spoke, the spirits of the ancestors sailed past on massive canoes, drumming and urging Moana onward. The girl's confidence returned!

At dawn, she sailed towards Te Fiti's island. Skilfully, she steered her boat to avoid Te Kā's jets of lava. She looked up – and there was Maui!

"I changed my mind, chosen one," he explained. "Go and save the world!"

As she faced Te Kā, Moana noticed a spiral on the monster's chest. Suddenly she understood. Te Kā and Te Fiti were the same! Losing her heart had turned the goddess into an angry demon.

"Let her come to me," Moana commanded the ocean.

The waves parted and the monster approached. Gently, Moana reached out and placed the heart into the spiral on Te Kā's chest. Instantly, the demon became a goddess again.

Both Moana and Maui knew it was time to say goodbye. After a final hug, Maui transformed into a hawk and flew away.

On Motunui, Moana's parents noticed that the withering plants were turning green again. And then they saw Moana, sailing over the reef and entering the lagoon! Everyone rushed to the shore to welcome her.

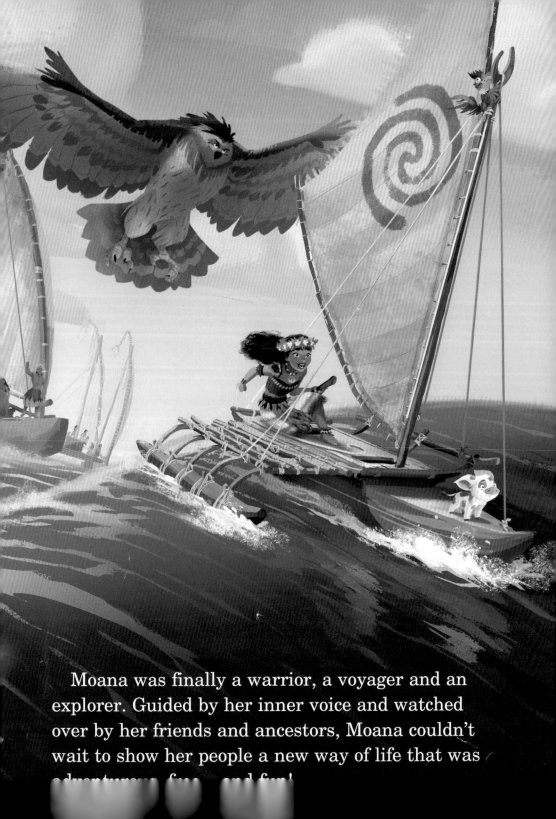

Moana was finally a warrior, a voyager and an explorer. Guided by her inner voice and watched over by her friends and ancestors, Moana couldn't wait to show her people a new way of life that was